I0556749

# everything but a novel

A Collection of Fiction
by Stacy Hinojos

OCYD Publishing

Published by OCYD Publishing
www.thesewords.blog

ISBN: 979-8-9912807-2-3

*To those who said I couldn't.*
*To those who said I wouldn't.*
*To those who said I shouldn't.*

*This is for you.*

*Preface*

The idea for Everything but a Novel: A Collection of Fiction originated following the completion of my second book of poetry. While I have long appreciated reading short stories, as an author, I find them particularly compelling due to the challenge of conveying complex worlds and emotions within a concise format.

After weeks of researching various compositions, I was motivated to see if I could write a range of fiction guided by defined short story parameters. The result of this endeavor is presented in this collection.

Stacy Hinojos

# Contents

## Six-Word Stories

• • • • •• • • • •• • • • •

Fiction stories written in six words.
No more, no less.

Ashes to ashes, no longer stars.

Sweetgrass lingered heavy on the breeze.

In the end, it was beautiful.

Enough. This would always be enough.

We are equally beautiful and evil.

We loved and loved some more.

There are no masters, only puppets.

The whisky burned bad memories away.

Loving her was enough for him.

Murder is a girl's best friend.

In the end, we all die.

Wouldn't it be nice to live?

Estate Sale. Dog up for adoption.

Breathing heavily, they stormed the beach.

She wore her mask so beautifully.

Forever, a curse we don't share.

Days like this should never end.

We return to the earth, dust.

The greatest curse was his love.

She stood at the edge, defeated.

Blood-soaked battlefields steaming with death.

Words hurt the soul for life.

Time disappears right before our eyes.

I'm the voice in your head.

He was aware but didn't care.


We are here together, forever more.


He always bit her with words.


Hope. That was all they had.


Life and love end, sometimes simultaneously.


She cursed him with divine words.


Heaven can wait one more day.


Giving everything, so they might live.

The rain came, washing life away.

Bang! The last thing she heard.

Minutes easily turned into beautiful moments.

How does love turn into this.

She escaped, with her heart intact.

Days grew colder, their love followed.

Breathing, he promised, was a gift.

Hearing the chanting, she joined in.

Twitterature

● ● ● ● ●● ● ● ● ●● ● ● ● ●

Fiction inspired by the popular social media app, Twitter.
These stories contain two hundred and eighty characters.
They were written on *Twitter Character Counter*
to ensure I followed the criteria.

### One

The little girl wearing the big red coat didn't know she was important, because most little girls weren't. Generations of people, years later, would watch her walk across a battlefield, her white flag waving in the breeze, wearing a smile as bright as the sun, to greet the enemy.

### Two

Sarah promised herself that she wouldn't cry as she quietly locked the front door behind her. "Looking back is dangerous," she thought to herself. "Whatever you do, don't glance into the rear-view mirror." She started the engine and realized how long the dirt road was to freedom.

### Three

She walked down the wood-lined dirt path at her nearby park. The scent of autumn encapsulated her. She breathed it all in. "I will be ok," she reassured herself. The leaves of orange, brown and gold danced in the breeze, reminding her to let go of everything that she didn't need.

## Four

The old photographs, yellowed and curling from age, fell like snow from a dusty leather album that had held them safely for over forty years. None of the smiling faces in the photos exist anymore. They are nothing more than ashes and bones, long lost stories that used to be told.

## Five

Burn down the house and everything within. Scream into the night about the garden that used to grow roses, but now only cultivates thorns. Dance in circles, cursing his name and all the lies he told. Watch the flames rise into the night sky and banish the love he doomed you with.

## Six

He spent two weeks lovingly trying to write a poem dedicated to her, as Valentine's Day neared. He soon realized that even the sweetest of poems looked angry, when scribbled in red pen across a pale pink construction paper heart. He felt foolish handing it to her, but she beamed.

### Seven

Every morning, she looked at herself in the mirror and said out loud, "I've got this. I can do hard things. I am enough. When in doubt, breathe. Believe." Yet, she didn't completely believe in herself, and she needed to. Her opinion of herself should be the only one that matters.

### Eight

As the record played, he spun her across the floor. They laughed and swayed to the song. She wanted to laugh like this forever, holding onto him, breathing him in. He never wanted to let her down or let her go. He pulled her closer and whispered all the things she longed to hear.

### Nine

What doesn't kill you makes you stronger. She knew that was a lie, as she lay there bleeding on the ground. It was dark and she knew no one would find her, especially as it began to rain. The cars were all zooming past, headlight beams bouncing off the trees right above her head.

## Ten

My horoscope told me to imagine everyone I've ever loved. Reluctantly, I did. I thought of the heartache, pain, lies, and betrayal. Then I took hold of the message. I remembered the love, joy, laughter, and the conversations I could never forget. Love can be a double-edged sword.

## Eleven

They said his chest contained a black heart. Dark through and through. Withered and wrinkled, and dry as a bone. Rumor had it that if he were stabbed, he wouldn't even bleed. And he'd walk across the street just to let you know that he hated breathing in the same air as you. RIP.

## Twelve

For some reason I remember the way my hand fit into yours, long ago when I was quite young. How soft and beautiful your skin felt against mine, and the distinctive sweet smell of your perfume that still lingers on your clothes as they lay in my closet, long after you have passed.

Short Poems

• • • •• • • • •• • • • •

Short poems written in
the author's eclectic style.

### *always sitting there*

the things you can't flee from
the hurt of the past
nightmares come true
are sitting there
waiting for a chance to return

### *As the Leaves*

As the leaves fall,
I wonder what the coming year will bring.

What will my eyes cry over?
What will my heart sing?

### *found*

in a world where hope is fading

but is full of beautiful filters

where conversations evade the deep end

and everything is plastic or fake

you somehow found me

and i found you

### *Garden Dance*

Remember the marigolds?

Or were they chrysanthemums?

Honestly, I cannot recall,

but I can still see the pattern of your dress,

and the way your bare feet danced,

as you planted them in the yard.

### *i carry*

i carry with me
pain of my ancestors

trauma ingrained
into the fiber of souls

### *In Search of Myself*

I lit my lantern

adjusted the flame

peered into the darkness

that spread before me

and slipped into the unknown

in search of myself

### *Missed*

You came to me in a dream.

It wasn't the first time.

I hope it's not the last.

We giggled and laughed

about the things that passed.

Dear boy,

you are missed.

## *My Silence*

My silence echoed loudly,
It rumbled through the halls,
Reaching every blessed ear,
Howling like a wolf,
Pleading for the moon to notice.

### *Throw Love*

I wonder,
most constantly,
how quickly you'd throw my love away,
if given half the chance to flee.

### *Truth Burns*

The whiskey doesn't burn
as much as it did last night.

I think it's because the
truth burns more today.

Dribbles

●　●　●　●●　●●　·　·　·　●●　　●　●　●　　●

Fiction written in fifty words.
No more, no less.

### Blessings Thrown

Child, your kind has long forgotten that they are the chosen ones. They each carry a lamp full of hope, peace, and love. Yet they have decided to waste their energy trying to douse their neighbor's light, instead of helping each other burn brighter. They casually throw away their blessings.

### Cost Me

Unfortunately, in the past I rarely listened to what made my heartbeat faster. I knew that I would miss experiencing things that might make me feel alive. I wouldn't allow myself to choose what permitted me to be happy, loved, and at peace. I know this has cost me dearly.

### Dearest Daughter,

Despite what you might think about yourself, you are not damaged goods. You are loved, and you are capable of loving. However, you must be willing to heal and trust again. Do the hard work and free yourself from the cage that was thrust upon you.

Love,
Mom

## *Parade for Breathing*

Shelby knew Danny didn't love her when only his feelings mattered. She wasn't allowed sadness, disappointment, happiness, or even pride. She was rarely taken into consideration. She was simply there, existing in the same realm, and in a constant state of anxiety. While he begged for a parade for breathing.

## *Perfected Ritual*

Centuries ago, women perfected the ritual of silent crying. Burying the rage and disbelief in what they witnessed, forever hurt by the experiences they endured. They clenched their fists under tables and practiced slow, deep breaths to calm their nerves. The wounds are sometimes visible, but most are buried deep.

## *Remembering Him*

Remembering him was easy. Your universe had been intertwined with every fiber of his being. You tried to absorb each second of every moment into a memory. A memory you could open like a gift on days that were cold and gray, when you needed sunshine to feel alive again.

### To the World,

It is not my job to make you love, or even like me. I have buried myself under false narratives, for far too long. It wasn't honest, and it wasn't real. I need to be who my heart is calling me to be. Unapologetically me.

Love,
Me

### True Colors

She couldn't believe what she saw, yet she wasn't surprised. Eventually people show their true colors, and we need to pay attention when they do. She had been taking careful mental notes and filing them away neatly. She knew that at some point she might need to open Pandora's box.

### Under the Surface

Despite the abundant sunlight on most of my days, there are times when there are storms brewing under the surface, like November gales on Lake Superior. I sit on the grass, eyes closed, face raised to the sun, praying to every god that I am not pulled under the waves.

Drabbles

• • • • •• • • •• • • • •

Fiction written in one hundred words.
No more, no less.

### *Another Day*

And so, it begins.

Another day of pain, as it holds my body hostage. Sheer exhaustion like I've just finished running the Boston Marathon and I've had no endurance training.

The throbbing in my head, reminding me that with each breath I take, I am that much closer to losing my mind.

Another day of being trapped in myself. I can barely get off the couch, but the kids need to be fed, and the house is falling apart.

So exhausted that my eyes burn, my vision blurred. I try not to cry.

Another day. I've made it another day.

## *Coffin Creeping*

At no point could I have predicted the anxiety of the situation. I sat cold with worry, on the examination table, waiting for the doctor to bring me the results that I knew wouldn't be welcomed.

My coffin was creeping closer to me than it lay a week ago. It didn't even try to disguise its heavy steps. Most people don't know that death has a very heavy step. Each footfall has a deafening echo that syncs with each beat of your heart.

Death was waiting on the other side of the door, listening with a smile on his face.

## *Diary Entry*

Dear Diary,

I have concluded that I might be the type of person who could kill a faux plant. There is a surprisingly good chance that I will accidentally say, "congratulations" at a funeral. I will acquire a case of giggles while receiving unwelcome news. On several occasions I have been known to walk around the airport with a trail of toilet paper stuck to the bottom of my shoe. I don't believe that this is the kind of flex I wanted to have at this stage of my life, cringeworthy embarrassment, but here we are. Simply me and messy.

## *Few Knew Her*

Simply put, people thought her dull. She was alone, but not lonely like others thought, because people rarely think. There was quiet satisfaction in her that others couldn't see. Calm, serene, peaceful.

She would walk through her days unfazed by what people thought. What difference did it make to her? Their ignorance was their own; it was not her job to correct them. And she didn't need to manufacture storms to appear interesting.

The few that found her fascinating knew her the best. They knew why she smiled when she was sad, and why she cried when she was happy.

## *Hospice Calls*

I cried again today when hospice called and said your name. They weren't alerted you died over the holiday. They apologized profusely.

The house is quiet without your oxygen machine. Your medications were removed from the fridge, the ones your nephews offered to buy.

The bedroom closet is half empty, so are the bathroom drawers. Your collectible figurines sit in a box at the end of the driveway, waiting to be picked up.

I don't believe I need more reminders that you've passed away. There is no conceivable way that the hole in my chest could allow me to forget.

## *Little Log Home*

Back in the woods, down an overgrown dirt road, stood a little log home, which was built with love.

It was held together with hopes and dreams. The more they hoped and dreamed, the stronger they became.

The tin roof kept them dry because their faith in each other was strong and unwavering.

When the winter winds of January came howling through, it stayed warm and cozy, because that tiny home was filled with laughter and kindness.

No, it did not look like much from the outside, but it was filled with everything two people who loved each other needed.

## *Old Letters*

I was cleaning out the bedroom closet yesterday when I came across the letters you wrote to me before we were married. I keep them in that antique wood box we found on the side of the road. The one we found that hot, humid August after the neighborhood garage sale. I sat on the floor, not as easily as I used to be able to, and I read every word you wrote. Do you know what those letters do to this heart of mine? They remind me that I was not only loved but cherished. I miss you, honey.

## *Pretty Words*

She wondered if she was capable of writing about pretty, ordinary things in life. Grass covered in dew and morning birds singing. The smell of old pine needles warmed by the sun and the sounds of waves landing on the shore. She would love to see softer, more beautiful words scrawled out on the page in front of her. Words she wrote. But the pain and anger she felt, the disappointments and fear, pushed those gentle words aside, and she could barely control the flow of her pen. For now, healing is important. There is time for pretty words later.

## *Raw, Then Healed*

When you write with unadulterated emotions, and they stare back at you from the page, it feels as raw as the first time you felt them, yet it's very healing. You are acknowledging that you lived through these experiences and felt something deeply. It's like accidentally stepping barefoot onto a glass shard. The prick of the sharp, jagged edge entering the underside of your foot, hobbling you as you bleed onto the floor. You try to sit down quickly to remove the shiny splinter, carefully cleaning and bandaging yourself, knowing that in a few days, you will be healed again.

## Long Poems

. . . .  .. . .  .. . .. .

Longer poems written in
the author's eclectic style.

### *Awakening of Spring*

Shivering, she stretches her limbs,
winter tumbling from her shoulders.
The ground will be beautiful covered in dew,
when tomorrow morning lifts.

Giving the sun a wave,
a smile on her lips,
she helps to unearth the
glorious shades of spring.

She sings out to her friends,
waking them with a lullaby.
Her voice weaves them a story,
with silvery spider's web.

The sun soon is yawning,
the winter chill is gone.
Dusk will soon be falling,
her forest friends need their sleep.

She falls into a deep slumber,
after turning off the day.
Tomorrow will be here soon enough,
and the fae will want to play.

## *Be a Poem*

My horoscope this morning read…

> Be a poem.

At first, I thought that was adorable.

> Be a poem.

So, I read it again.

> Be a poem.

It didn't say anything else, just…

> Be a poem.

What on earth does that even mean?

> Be a poem?

I went to a quiet place to think
about every poem I ever read.

> The happy, the sad.
> Words of love, hope, joy, despair.

I stayed in my quiet place to think
about every poem I ever wrote.

> The sad, the happy.
> Words of despair, joy, hope, love.

Yes, be a poem.

### *Begins Again*

Stretching out my wings to fly,
I have learned to survive another
cycle of wintered emotions.

I buried them with the spring seeds,
and they awoke with the summer sun,
gentle breeze, and warm rains.

Autumn has just begun,
and the falling leaves guide my
withered emotions away from me.

Winter will be here soon,
along with the snow,
freezing me in place.

Then it begins again.

### *Drifted to Sleep*

Watching myself,
from up above,
pill bottles scattered,
from wall to wall.

Booze,
the whiskey
in particular,
made me feel brave.

Today is as good,
as any other day,
just make the
landing stick.

No longer able
bear the weight,
of the world
on my shoulders.

I laid down,
wrapped myself
in a blank,
and drifted to sleep.

### *Forever Moment*

The sun shining
Clear blues skies
Soft breeze
Waves crashing over mica sand

You and your daddy
Wearing your favorite hats
Holding hands
Walking to the water's edge

I have never felt happier
Or more filled with love
Then I did on that
Warm April day

Him teaching you how
To build sand castles
You dancing and
Laughing in the tide

I took snapshot
After snapshot
In my mind
I wanted this moment forever

### *Ice Cold*

He lies alone
In the dark
Ice cold

No one to hold his hand
No one to kiss his forehead
No one to snuggle

We have said our goodbyes
But we haven't let go
We can't let go

But he lies alone
In the dark
Ice cold

## *Imperfect Amelia*

The sun rose perfectly
From behind perfect clouds
Above the perfect houses
Resting on their perfect lawns.

While perfect wives
Wake their perfect children
And perfect husbands
Rush off in their perfect suits.

Except for Amelia.

As she sat on her imperfect couch
In her imperfect home
Watching all the perfect things rush by
She hoped to remain imperfect.

### *Made Me Love Again*

You made me believe in myself,
you made me believe in us.
You loved me for who I was,
and who I could be again.

You found me in the darkness,
a darkness you also knew.
A place of loneliness,
a place of brokenness.

You reached out to me,
through the vast unknown.
You risked what was left
of your own heart.

You cared for me,
you took the time to mend me.
You fixed my broken heart,
and you made me love again.

### *My Wish for You*

To love, be loved, and continue to love,
through any pain your heart might feel.

To be surrounded by blue skies,
never grey.

To feel the sun warm
your back and face.

To release your feelings like a balloon,
just let them float away.

To dance among the fireflies
under a star filled sky.

To remember those sweet moments
during those difficult days.

To feel my embrace,
or a kiss upon your face.

To feel the power of lighting when
it races across a midnight sky.

To walk through the autumn leaves
as children laugh.

To watch the birds take flight,
singing their journey away.

To always have shelter over your head,
and warm clothes to wear.

To have food on your table,
with plenty to spare.

To have comfort at night
during those lonely times.

To have plenty of friends to
support you during the day.

This is what I wish for you.

### *Nature's Friends*

Yes, I talk to the trees,
the whip-o-wills,
and the bumblebees.

I listen as the crows caw,
the hummingbirds buzz,
and the mourning doves coo.

I share stories with mice,
while petting the squirrels,
and sitting among the moss.

I walk with the deer in the morning,
wave to the owl,
and sing along with the robin.

I hide treats for the porcupine,
while watching the foxes frolic,
and breathe in the warm pine.

## *Nightmares End*

Good luck finding me in the shadow, honey.
Good luck finding me when I'm dead.
You're no good at all this long-distance running,
With feet sinking in the sand.

You're only a danger in your own head, honey.
You don't have what it takes to be a man.
Shame rarely falls upon thin shoulders,
No one expected much from you anyway.

The night is getting colder, sugar.
You feel me in the shadows yet?
Crawling closer to your pretty face, baby.
Tonight, your nightmares end.

## *Not My Own*

These stories are not always my own.

Many of the words I write have been shared with me.

Sacred connections between reader and writer.

Dark heavy words, hanging with tears.

Words angry and sharp, dipped in poison.

Dreams full of love, waiting and wanting.

These words sit silently.

We stare at each other until we grieve their meanings, and then I set them free.

Free to roam on the page.

### *Peace in Silence*

Is there really peace in the silence
that surrounds me late at night,
and into the early morning light?

My mind rests unsettled,
full of noise and chaos,
it makes my blood race.

A reel of conversations plays,
the old and new,
my heart once again black and blue.

No, peace does not find me,
no matter how I try,
I cannot mute what resides in my mind.

### *Pondering and Wondering*

Darkness rolled in,
as it often does this time of night.

The day grows older.
Quieter.
Wiser.

The blueness overshadowed by black,
temperature change slight.

You sit.
Watching.
Pondering

Wondering why all this exists.

The paths of all those before you,
wondered the same.

### *Shine Down*

Oh, shine down
Shine down on me
Oh, shine down
Like the sun through the trees.

Oh, hold me
Hold me tightly
Oh, hold me
Till time stops following.

Oh, shine down
Shine down on me
Oh, shine down
Like the sun through the trees.

Oh, keep me
Keep me near
Oh, keep me
Always and forever.

Oh, shine down
Shine down on me
Oh, shine down
Like the sun through the trees.

## Micro Stories

• • • • •• • • • •• • •• • •

Fiction written in three hundred words or less.

### *Breathing Should Be Easy*

For six years she didn't breathe, not properly, at least. Breathing should be automatic, easy. She knew if she exhaled fully, she wouldn't be able to hold in all the words she longed to say. She might start yelling, but she might never stop.

So, she held her breath when they were in the same room together. She would only respond to questions by shaking her head "yes" or "no," which suited him, because he didn't require long conversations with her.

But once that airplane landed in a country 4,000 miles away, she took a deep breath, and she exhaled long and slow. Her entire body felt lighter. She took another long, slow, deep breath and let it out as slowly as she could. Exhaling the anxiety and anger that had been building inside, weighing her down like concrete boots. She no longer felt like she was suffocating; she finally felt like she was alive.

She smiled because breathing was finally easy.

## *Childhood Dreams Lived*

Even as a small girl in a very small town, Mara had always dreamed big. It isn't that she didn't appreciate the area she grew up in, or the natural beauty she was surrounded by, but her eyes longed to see the sights of the entire world.

With her bags packed and her goodbyes said, this was her chance to venture off into lands of indescribable beauty. Places with impressive architecture, and far-flung cultures. Great cities full of neon lights and museums. Small villages complete with ancient churches and historical sites thousands of years old.

She wanted this change of scenery to be accompanied by wine and food that changed her taste buds, locales that looked like they belonged in a movie, and foreign languages that melted her soul. She wanted to experience what she had only read about in her dad's old National Geographic magazines.

She took one last look around her bedroom, noticing the dusty outlines of all the maps that had once hung on her walls, and she shut the door to her childhood dreams, because now it was the time to live them.

## *Corked Bottles*

During group therapy, someone asked me what I do with my anger. "What do you mean?" I responded. "I do what everyone else does. I bottle it up, seal it with a cork, and ignore it." I took a deep breath and continued talking because there was an awkward silence.

"Once in a while, someone or something comes along and shakes the bottle." I pretend to shake an invisible bottle to enhance my point. "It's not always on purpose, the shaking, but it definitely challenges the strength of the cork!" I laugh the way I always do when I don't want to discuss difficult things anymore.

The therapist takes their cue and delivers a speech on healthy coping mechanisms,
while I sit there and think about all the bottles stored under my bed.

## *Dancing in the Rain*

I stood in the doorway drinking my coffee as the storm rolled in, darkening the sky, rumbling with the thunder of a hundred mustangs galloping across the plains. The wind, gently blowing through my hair, caressed my cheek, leaving me with a smile on my face.

The rain started to tap dance on the ferns that grew alongside the covered porch, and the trees started to sway with the wind. The smell of damp earth filled my soul with a reminder that I was alive, and that I belonged here.

The puddles began to swell, beckoning me to jump and splash. I don't know if I was daydreaming, but I heard a voice whisper, "Connect with your inner child, they are still a part of you! Stand in the rain and frolic like Gene Kelly in that old movie you used to watch with your grandma. Live your life while you can!"

I put my cup of coffee down, ran down the steps, and I started to twirl in the rain with my arms stretched out, laughing with the crows.

### *Lack of Words*

Yes, it's messy, this life we live. It almost always is. It's confusing and wondrous, and so exhausting. The constant up and down each hour can bring, not to mention the unpredictability that others bring into our lives.

When we are perplexed or overwhelmed, people might say, "Just talk about it."

Friends hug you and say, "Tell us how you feel."

But sometimes I can't. Sometimes I don't have the words I long to say, which is weird, because I know words. I possess buckets of words. Plus, I know I have a voice, because I hear myself; in my head I hear myself, so why can't I just talk?

Granted, my voice is not always strong enough, or deliberate enough, but I do have a voice. I need to exercise it. I should perform so many repetitions a day to strengthen it. Maybe I should study a thesaurus to gain more words that could land a gentler, or even heavier, blow.

Why is it so damn hard to say the things we've all heard with our own ears before? Delicate things. Hurtful things. Burdensome things. Angry things. Beautiful things.

"I lost my job."
"I'm moving."
"I love you."
"I'm pregnant."
"Your mother died."
"There was an accident."
"I want a divorce."
"I have cancer."

Because once we say those words, they become real things. They are alive. We must face them, even if we knew it was coming. And once we hear those words live and breathe, there is now a blip in the timeline of before they were spoken and after.

So, I'm trying to find my voice and the most perfect of words to tell you...goodbye.

## *Not Enough Silver Lining*

I do often wonder what life would have been like if you hadn't come along. I think about all the pain you caused me, while trying to spot the silver lining. However, it feels that everything attached to you comes flooding back in muddy waves, trying to drown me yet again.

There are flickers, somewhere in the distance, of things that were honestly thoughtful and loving. But those bright sparks are quickly dimmed and are few and far between. I had once dreamed of a life of happiness and joy with you, yet all that was swept away by quick tides I never saw coming.

I finally had to accept defeat in the end. No matter how many conversations or arguments we had, we were not meant to see eye-to-eye. We had different definitions for what love entailed, and unfortunately neither of us were right.

## *Short-Term Happiness*

It was late afternoon, and the sun was starting to peek out from the grey clouds. It had been raining gently most of the morning, with a nice breeze, perfect napping weather. Sam was jet-lagged, and Chloe had been working late at the bar, so she was happy he wanted to rest.

"I love you," Sam said.

"Don't be cruel," Chloe responded.

"I'm not trying to be," he replied. "I do love you. I have always loved you. I just can't allow myself to love you because I know I will hurt you."

Sam had wanted, for years, to tell Chloe the truth about the way he felt. Their timing was always off, life continued to spin out of control, and opportunity never knocked.

Sam continued, "I know it like I know the sun will rise tomorrow, even if the skies are cloudy and grey. I know it like I know Christmas will always disappoint me. I know it like I know your own heart. I don't wish to hurt you."

Chloe rolled over so she could look into Sam's eyes. He smiled at her.

"So, despite my being fully and excusably in love with you, I am sacrificing your short-term happiness and my possible long-term happiness, because in the end I hurt everyone. Including myself. We all know it. Especially you." Sam's smile faded as he finished, waiting to hear what Chloe had to say.

"Sam," Chloe heard a small sigh leave his lips. "I love you, too. Maybe short-term happiness would be worth it in the end."

## *The Fairy Tale of Hush*

Once there was a story that needed to be told, but alas, there was no one who could tell it.

The entire village of Hush tried to speak the words that longed to be shared; however, their tongues could only stutter or flutter. On a perfectly mediocre sunny day, as days tend to be, an unknown woman danced through the quiet village of Hush.

The woman wore a flowing gown made of gold and white silk, and bells were woven into her auburn hair. She had a silver voice, which carried her poems and songs through the air. To say that the whole village stopped to stare was not merely an exaggeration. They gathered all around her when she stopped at the village well.

She looked up, graciously, as she took a ladle full of water to her lips and whispered a gentle spell. For she had known upon entering the little village that it was under the cruel spell of her sister. She swallowed the cool water, quenching her deep thirst, and the incantation that had fallen over the village, fractured in an instant.

The village rejoiced and sang out their praises, finally able to speak again and tell the story of the stranger in gold and white and her sister dressed head-to-toe in black.

### *The Ghost at Pine and 4th*

The old green house on the corner of Pine and 4th, all higgledy-piggledy in assembly, had walls filled with coal dust and old newspapers. Every wall of every room was yellowed from hundreds of smoked cigarettes. Roaming throughout the house was the former owner, now deceased, who once proclaimed his undying love for his house, saying on his death bed that he would never leave. He was a man of his word.

Now, most ghosts won't bother you, they are either curious or simply shy. Some are watchers and tricksters waiting to swipe and hide your house keys when you aren't looking. However, there are a small percentage who are nothing if not vile and cruel. They will do anything, or almost anything, to get you to leave.

I will not confirm or deny the rumors that float around town, but I've had my own experiences there. I will give you this warning, that when the owner's dog barks and growls, your arms are suddenly covered in goose bumps on a summer's day, and the hair stands up on the back of your neck, you might want to run and hide.

## *Washed Away*

He watched her strip bare and walk into the ocean for the second day in a row. Her body was covered in welts, bruises, and deep scratches. She wouldn't wince, despite the saltwater lapping at her wounds. The wounds he created.

She would wade out three feet from shore, walking backwards, so she could maintain eye contact with him, never blinking. It unnerved him, making him shudder.

She dipped below the surface, for no more than a few seconds, to drown her pain. Slowly she would rise out of the surf, lock eyes with him again, and walk towards her clothes that lay in a pile on the sand.

He tried to bring a towel towards her, but she jumped, like a rabbit caught stealing baby lettuce leaves growing in a garden. Fear racing through her body, she would quickly get dressed.

By the fifth day he wondered if she would ever forgive him.

By the seventh day she allowed him to wrap a towel around her shoulders.

On the tenth day he thought he saw a slight smile on her lips as she slowly submerged her body beneath the waves. A minute later she didn't resurface. Two minutes later he began to hear his heart beating in his ears. He stared out into the spot she once stood, and he started running into the waves, feeling sick to his stomach.

Just like that, she was gone. Washed away like she never existed.

## Micro Fiction

• • • • •• • • •• • • • •

Fiction written in three hundred
to five hundred words.

## *Comfortable Quiet*

They lay in bed, surrounded by the late morning sunshine and dust motes dancing in the rays that filtered through the partially turned blinds. Rebecca enjoyed these moments with Jack. It was easy, and it felt natural. "Comfortable quiet," Jack had called it. Rebecca hoped that this would be a forever feeling, but sometimes doubt would creep into her mind as she traced the visible scars on her wrists and arms.

Jack noticed this small movement of hers out of the corner of his eye, but he did not move his head to watch her. He knew if they were together for twenty years or more, he would never hear everything her body ached to tell him. Pain, he understood, has individuality. Even shared experiences would be felt differently by those who shared them.

Jack put his book down, looked over at Rebecca and said, "Your pain is beautiful." He gently took her left arm in his right hand so he could see what she was tracing, and he took over, slowly tracing where the cuts once bled with his left index finger.

Rebecca looked at Jack, tears in her eyes, unable to speak. He wanted her to know that he wasn't pressing for her to talk. If one's heart wasn't ready, pushing them into an uncomfortable position wouldn't make it any easier.

"Rebecca, I know I may never be able to fathom what has happened in your life before we met. I know you may never be able to tell me details of your life. I don't expect you to share those events with me. But whatever happened, made you the person sitting next to me. And I think, for whatever it is worth, that you are the most beautiful person in my world, external wounds, internal wounds, and all. Thank you for sharing the parts of you, you are comfortable with, to me."

Rebecca shed a few tears while exhaling years of hurt, pulled Jack into her embrace, and whispered, "Thank you, Jack. Thank you."

## *Death's Secrets*

You often hear people say, very dramatically, "My world fell apart! The rug was pulled out from underneath me! Nothing will ever be the same again!" The exaggeration in their voice, the pain in their eyes sinks into my soul. I used to be able to understand, I could feel my heart being pulled in commiseration. It's not that I'm now unsympathetic, or that I lack empathy, but I lack energy for their predicament.

For me, my life has been otherworldly. It was as if someone dropped an unpronounceable drug into my drink and dragged me into another world where they strapped me into a roller coaster from hell. As soon as I staggered off, and threw up, they pushed me down a never-ending flight of stairs, and I'm still falling to this day. I hope I don't pull you down with me, please forgive me if I do.

This has been my punishment for centuries, courtesy of my misdeed of trying to rebury the secrets and lies of those who had crossed over into the next plane. I thought that it was a noble occupation, but someone higher up, or lower down, did not agree.

So, I sit here, loathing the truth that death brings to those who are already heartbroken and full of grief. For each undisclosed truth that is released to those left behind, it will cause a unique set of emotions to erupt. But for most humans, the secrets will be painful, and some will open old wounds. Why add salt to already gaping wounds? Secrets should remain secret, buried alongside the dead six feet under and cold.

After all these years of watching others crumble once the departed soul's private dealings have been unleashed, I am still surprised at how some secrets truly are deadly.

### *Hide and Seek*

A little boy sat on a hill one night, far beyond his bedtime, and he looked up at the moon and sang, "Man, man, man in the moon, please come down and play with me."

The man in the moon looked down at the boy and said, "It's far beyond your bedtime; you should be fast asleep in your bed."

"Oh please," said the little boy in his sweet small voice, "I promise I'll go to sleep after we play hide-and-seek."

The man in the moon smiled because he did love to play hide-and-seek. "We can play one round, but then you must go to sleep."

The man in the moon started to count to thirty, and the little boy ran to hide.

But the boy could not decide where he wanted to hide.

First, he tried to hide behind a tree, but the trunk was not very wide.

Then he tried to hide behind the cat, but the cat kept moving around.

Finally, he hid inside the doghouse, despite the dog trying to sleep.

The man in the moon watched all of this between his moonbeam fingers, and he tried not to laugh.

"27...28...29...30! Here I come," shouted the man in the moon.

First the man in the moon looked behind the tree. "No little boy here," he said. And the little boy laughed.

Then he looked behind the cat, who would not stop moving around. "No little boy here," he said. And the little boy laughed.

Finally, the man in the moon said, "I know, I'll look in the doghouse!"

"I found you," shouted the man in the moon! And the little boy laughed and laughed.

"Now, we've played a game of hide and seek, so now it is time for bed." And the man in the moon picked up the little boy with his moon beam arms, and swung him side to side, while humming a lullaby. The little boy quickly fell asleep.

### *Putting Fires Out to Heal*

There are stories from our past, which are still too hot to hold within our hands. They live in our hearts and minds burning, as more fuel is occasionally added to the flames. It is difficult, sometimes impossible; to dig those emotions out so we might be able to extinguish them.

Flashes of memories. A word spoken harshly. A familiar scent. Feelings, even small, can stir those flames. Why were we not equipped with extinguishers, or even a bucket of sand, the fancy red ones you see on a tour of a stately home, to put these fires out?

I try to put into place those coping mechanisms I learned in therapy. The exercises to reassure myself that I am ok. That I do not live in the past. I am looking at myself in the mirror, older, but not necessarily any wiser. Although I need to carry some of the blame now, because I know better.

But I know myself. I know I repeat patterns. I know I will sit there and tell myself that this is a "me" problem and that I am far too sensitive. "You are overthinking this. It is a simple overreaction to a situation that is just a misunderstanding, an overinterpretation. Just let them off the hook this one time, because even though you have talked about this, this really is a me issue, and I need to just swallow my pride and get over it."

I know deep down that we are all hurting from the fires within us. That we struggle day in and day out with healing. Healing is challenging work, and it is scary. We convince ourselves we do not need it because we know what is wrong within ourselves, and we can fix it. Sometimes we ignore the fact that we do, in fact, need therapy. This adds fuel to the flames, but it is easier than booking that damn appointment.

So, while I try to find myself a fancy red bucket of sand, I hope you find yourself a fire extinguisher. I think we can all agree that these flames are burning too brightly.

## Ride Home

Sometimes, after work you would ask if I would like a ride home. This did not happen every night we worked together, only when you needed someone to understand you, or if you felt that I needed some time to think about my life. In mutual brokenness, we would sit in your car, mostly silent, as we smoked and listened to the radio. We would drive around town until we were ready to face what was waiting for us at home.

A couple of times, we sat by the lake as the moon rose over those dark waves. We sat there and breathed in the night air, wondering about all the things that we did not have answers for, even when we lied to ourselves.

We cried together once and screamed into the somber dusk that embraced us, knowing that we did not have to explain ourselves or apologize for the bitter words that tumbled from our lips. We looked at each other afterwards, started laughing at the absurdity of it all, and ran back to the car, out of breath and coughing.

When I decided to move away, because I had no other options, we promised we would stay in touch. We knew we were lying, and we forgave each other easily. I wondered for years if you were doing ok, that you found what you needed out of life, because I knew I had not.

Two decades later, you were asking for my phone number, and we would talk for hours as if no time had passed. When you told me of the heartache you faced and the challenges you had ahead of you, I knew you would not be in my life for much longer. I knew that I was borrowing time and that my privilege would be revoked without warning.

Unfortunately, I was right. I miss you, friend.

## Sudden Fiction

• • • •  •• • • • •• • •  • •

Fiction written with at least seven hundred fifty words,
but under one thousand words.

### Midwest Goodbyes

Dani was just another face in a crowd. Shoulder to shoulder with other nameless folks, walking aimlessly to unknown destinations. The privacy of being one more body in a big city. She enjoyed the peacefulness of being invisible. For instance, there were no forced conversations about the weather.

"Didja hear about those storms rollin' in? Ya better get that snowblower of yours ready because I saw those geese huddling in the field yesterday."

There could be no hushed discussions about someone's health, failed marriage, or secrets being spread to the point that they were no longer secrets.

"Didja hear Aunt Francine's gout is acting up again? Of course, I blame your Uncle Ralph and that secretary of his."

There were no obligatory good mornings, hellos, or the ever popular, "Well Dani, d'jeet"?

On the rare occasion though, if she tripped over an uneven spot in the sidewalk or bumped into a stranger in the store, an "ope" would escape from her lips. It would sometimes make her smile. Ope. A little phrase from home that she could not do away with, no matter where she travelled, no matter how far she moved away.

Rumor had it that she could save herself countless hours every year, simply by not tapping into her Midwest mannerisms. That meant no more greeting everyone with a smile and a silently mouthed "hi." No more nod of the head in silent recognition as you passed in the hallway. No more fingers raised on a steering wheel as you drove by someone you have known since birth. It now meant pushing through the crowd instead of saying "ope," "excuse me," or even a, "can I scooch by ya real quick?" Dani is certain she has saved herself at least a dozen hours by no longer taking part in the traditional Midwest goodbye.

Her father was the champion of the Midwest Goodbye, and it was always on full display at every family function, but especially on Christmas Eve. Her mother would tell her and her sister, "Say goodbye to everyone quick; we gotta get home before Santa beats us there. And don't forget the hugs!" Her father would then begin to swagger from room to room, giving all his siblings, aunts, uncles, cousins, and his parent's neighbors a warm hug or handshake and exchanging one last quick story.

"Do yous remember da time when George there forgot to use da hand brake when he parked on Blakely Hill by the cemetery? I thought for sure he was gonna send that truck down into Pastor Wood's house."

"Those cookies were burned like the dickens! Still ate 'em though. Worst stomachache ever!"

"Oh ya, that was Sarah's fault all right. Remember, I'm the good kid in the family."

Thirty minutes later, someone would hand him a beer or another brandy slush, because "his storytelling voice must be feeling dry," they would say. He would gladly take it, and head into another room to continue saying goodbye. But by this time, Dani could start feeling the sweat drip down her back beneath her new fluffy Christmas sweater that was slowly getting damp under her heavy winter coat. Fidgeting, she would look up at her mother, who was in a struggle of her own to escape, after being cornered by grandma who was going on and on about the neighbor boys and their snowmobiles racing through the corn field. Grandma was also exceptionally good at the Midwest goodbye.

"Girls, why don't you head out to the car," their mother always thought this would help move their father along, but they knew better. She quickly shooed them out of the kitchen door into the freezing night air before grandma could grab hold of them, taking them hostage in another round of Midwest charades. "Bill the girls are melting, let's go!" she would shout. Giggling, Dani and her sister would race each other up and down the driveway, seeing who could slide across the icy patches the fastest, wondering if they had time to build a snowman. Meanwhile their father would be regaling loved ones about the great deal he got on the new snow tires down at the Fleet Farm.

"Just in the nick of time! Didja hear about those storms movin' in?"

Fifteen minutes later, mother would open the kitchen door to check on them, "Girls, get out of the snowbank, you're wearing your Sunday shoes! Bill I'm starting the car!"

By this time, neither Dani nor her sister could feel their toes, so they gratefully hopped into the car, knowing their warm breath would start freezing on the windows. "Here girls, take my purse and the crockpot." Dani's mother slid into the driver's seat, and started the car, sighing, from too much politeness and conversation. "Are you girls excited for Christmas?" she would ask, as she turned on the radio.

Ten minutes later, they knew they were leaving for real when they heard that old kitchen door swing open, wind catching the wreath, and heard grandpa shout, "Merry Christmas, son. Be sure to watch out for da deer!"

As Dani stood there at the corner, waiting for the little man to turn green, watching the many cars drive by, she started smiling to herself. Maybe she would book a trip home for Christmas this year.

## *Rainbows*

The early morning sun slowly rose above the high rises across the street and chased away the shadows in Grant's apartment. He sat on his brown leather couch, with only the refrigerator hum keeping him company. A glass of whisky sat on a coffee table in front of him. It had been sitting there since he poured it the night before, and he had stared at it without blinking for several hours.

He continued to breathe in the stale air, and watched the sunlight flood the living room. He hadn't showered in two days, and he couldn't remember the last time he swallowed food. Despite being more exhausted than he had ever felt, he couldn't manage to close his eyes and sleep.

Grant looked down at the glass sitting on the coffee table. He thought if he drank it, the whisky might help keep his eyes closed. But he was too tired to even pick that glass up and put it to his lips. She had given him the set of crystal whisky glasses for his birthday last year, as he had only one left from his father's old cocktail set. She carefully placed the antique glass from his father onto the shelf next to his dad's photograph. "Now, you'll have that glass forever."

Zoe had always been thoughtful like that. She had always gone out of her way to show that she loved somebody. "Had," Grant whispered to himself. "She had just been here, how is it that she's gone?" She had left the world unexpectedly and it was too soon for Grant to start picking up the pieces. "What a senseless, stupid waste!" Grant grabbed the glass full of whisky off the coffee table and launched it across the room in anger. It broke against the wall next to the shelf that held his father's photograph and glass, knocking them both off the wall.

"Damn it! Why the hell did I do that?!?" Grant walked over to the now broken shelf. He grasped his father's picture, wiping the frame with the back of his sleeve. He smiled down at his dad. "You would have loved Zoe. Everybody did."

The sunlight caught hold of the crystal shards that were now strewn across the floor and dispersed mini rainbows across the room. Grant smiled again. Zoe loved rainbows. She would ask Grant to walk with her to the park after every storm just in case there was a rainbow to spot. She would jump in every puddle they came across, laughing and grinning at him. Zoe had confided in Grant that her mother used to race her outside after every storm to see who could spot the rainbow first. The last time they had gone out together, her mother died that evening. Zoe was only nine years old. "I swear I can feel that my mom is with me when we go outside after a storm. It heals a little part of me."

Grant sat on the floor, looking around the living room at all the beautiful colors. His grief seemed to feel a little lighter at that moment, and he couldn't be sure, but it felt like Zoe was hugging him. It was then that Grant caught sight of his father's old glass, laying there. He was almost afraid to pick it up. "Huh, not a scratch or a chip." Grant carefully placed the glass in the sink and grabbed the vacuum from the closet in the hall.

He cautiously picked up the large pieces of glass, wondering what Zoe would have said at his outburst, especially at him breaking something. His mind was so preoccupied that he didn't notice the large shard embedded in the carpet, and he stepped on it.

For the second time that day, Grant unleashed a string of profanities, mostly down to his own carelessness. He hobbled over to the hallway to where the First Aid Kit lived, and he hobbled back over to the couch. Grant sat down and lifted his left leg over his right knee to inspect the damage he caused himself. "Not too bad."

He opened the box and searched for the tweezers. He eventually found it underneath what Grant first thought was a booklet of common medical emergencies, but when he looked in the box again for a bandage, he realized that it was an envelope.

Grant ignored his injured foot and looked down at the envelope in his hands. It looked like the ones Zoe would special order from the print shop down the block. Grant flipped the envelope over and saw his name, written in Zoe's neat penmanship. With his hands shaking, he quickly opened it up.

*Dearest Grant,*

*If you find this letter it means you've hurt yourself again, either while cutting onions or stepping on a piece of glass. Maybe you are doing your annual, "hunt for the expiration dates on everything in the apartment" while making a list of everything you need to replace.*

*I just want you to know that I love you a great deal. You've made me a stronger, more loving person. I look forward to the day that we get married and celebrate with all our friends and family. All two of them!*

*Thank you for all the rainbows.*
*Zoe*

Grant, softly laughing with tears in his eyes, read the letter to himself again. "Oh Zoe, my precious girl. Thank you for making me believe in the healing part of rainbows."

## *The End*

With each breath Angel took, she somehow gained strength to continue towards her dream. Her heart longed to stand in the cold, clear, blue waters of that great big lake back home. The thought of being able to see those waves roll onto the shoreline welcoming her to her final resting place, carried her through the dark days of chemotherapy and radiation treatments. Those same thoughts would now bring her soul calm to face the end of her life.

She gazed out the window, watching another March snowstorm rage on. The limbs of pine trees were snapping under the weight of snow and ice. "I just need to make it until June, that's all I want. That's all I need. I've never asked or expected much in my life, but back home is where I need to be. That's where I want to say good-bye."

Her doctors advised Angel to put her affairs in order and take this opportunity to say goodbye to those she loved, because they would be surprised if she would be able to usher in the month of April. She refused because that felt like she was giving in. She knew cancer would absorb her, but she wanted to be the one to say, "Ok, I'm finished." She was more than stubborn, and she was twice as determined. Her doctors knew she was, yet they were all surprised when she sailed through April, tired, but not any worse for wear.

By mid-May she was the most tired she'd ever been, but she started to finalize her, "Great Goodbye." Each time she completed an item on her to-do list, she felt more certain she would make it home.

She found the perfect cabin, where she could host all her most important people. She phoned a local caterer to arrange all the meals to be made and delivered, so everyone could relax together. She even had a friend design a white gown, embroidered with small sunflowers, that she would proudly wear. Now the time had come for everyone to head North, she was ready to let go of everything earthly.

If Angel had been uncomfortable on the four-hour ride, she didn't show it. She smiled the whole journey, pointing out spots here and there to her family and friends, and spinning stories that made everyone laugh. Angel gasped when she caught sight of her beloved lake. She took a deep breath, inhaling the warm pines and the water, and felt exhilarated.

For three nights and three days Angel and her crew filled their days with laughter, swimming, campfires, delicious food, and stargazing. Everyone thought that maybe the doctors were wrong, that somehow a miracle took place once Angel's toes had touched that beautiful water. But that evening, Angel's final rally began, the final burst of energy right before the "big finish." And while everyone around her began to wear their sadness on their faces, she wouldn't let it rain on her parade.

The next morning Angel woke up before the sun had peeked its head over the water and asked for help getting her white gown on. She knew that she didn't have much time, and she wanted to enjoy one last sunrise. But before she could do that, she wanted to make sure that each person there knew how important they were to her.

Angel had carefully saved flower arrangements people had sent her while she had been ill. She dried and pressed dozens of petals and leaves and mixed them into the paper pulp she made from the cards people had mailed her. She'd meticulously labeled each sheet of paper with the giver's name. "Yellow roses from Beth. Forget-Me-Nots from Sam. Sunflowers from Aunt Birdie." Angel then spent the week before the trip North writing letters to those people. Letters of love and inspiration, to help them through the grief they would soon meet.

Angel called each person one-at-a-time into her room to hand deliver their letter, instructing them that she wished for them to read their letter when the moment felt right for them to read it. She allowed each person a chance to say what they might need to say, or just to give them a moment to shed tears together.

When the last letter had been delivered, Angel asked to be carried outside to the water's edge, where a lounge chair had been placed so she could watch the sun rise, and feel the warmth on her face one last time. She smiled when she spotted where they had placed her chair and exclaimed how beautiful the sandy path looked lined with candles and torches. They bundled blankets around her to make her as comfortable and warm as possible.

With the waves lightly lapping at the shoreline, the sun slowly greeted Angel, lighting her relaxed, now glowing face. She had realized her dream, the most important in her life. While everyone was standing and sitting around her, holding onto each other, watching the sun fully reveal itself, Angel closed her eyes, and breathed her last breath.

A Short Story

● ● ● ● ● ● ● ● ● ● ● ● ● ● ●

Fiction written in at least one thousand words,
but no more than five thousand.

## *A Friend's Visit*

Richard knew, as soon as he walked through the door, that things were not all well within her life and her "happy" modest home. He heard the kettle bubbling away in the kitchen. He smelled the freshly baked cookies. If he strained his ears, he could hear the small sounds of a baby cooing merrily in the backroom. But when Anya embraced him, a look of relief showed on her face, and it made him melancholy.

"Hello, old chap," her husband called out. "How was the flight?"

"Oh, you know…" Richard trailed off. "You remember my girlfriend, Phoebe?"

"Hello, good to see you again!" His friend Nigel was always overly cheerful with company, but he had seen the way Nigel talked to his wife when he thought no one was in earshot.

He watched Anya's face tighten each time her husband talked. She noticed he was watching her, and she gave him a small smile. They had been friends for five years now; he had known her husband for twice as long. He was the reason they had met in the first place.

Anya had jokingly said at one point, "If this marriage ends in divorce, it will be your fault."

He thought of that now and felt his heart sink because he recognized that this was how Anya's marriage would end. And he knew by the look on her face that she knew it too.

"I'll help you with the tea," he said, looking at her. "Phoebe, why don't you go look at the baby? You've been talking non-stop about seeing him for weeks now." Phoebe followed Nigel into the backroom.

"Well, motherhood looks good on you. Marriage however..." He was always direct with her; Anya always appreciated that about Richard.

"Is it that obvious?"

"Yes. But maybe it's because you know you don't have to pretend around me."

"That is probably true. I do appreciate you and Phoebe coming for a visit, I know you're both so busy at work. How are the negotiations going? Do you miss me playing the bad cop?" As Anya started to laugh, she knew Nigel was about to enter the kitchen. She knew it bothered Nigel that her and Richard were much closer than he had ever been with their friend.

"There you two are! Phoebe might just sneak out with the baby in her handbag today if we're not careful. I'll take the tea in." Nigel picked up the tea tray and carried it out.

"I can barely get a moment without him invading every

conversation or activity," Anya whispered to Richard. "It's as if he doesn't trust me to breathe. Even when I am alone."

"You know, you don't have to stay here. I could talk to Jax about rehiring you. You and the baby could stay with Phoebe and me until you found a place."

"I could, and I would, but I think he's already talked to lawyers."

"You mean, he talked to his brother," responded Richard. Anya rolled her eyes and laughed. Every time Nigel was in trouble or thought trouble was following him, he'd call on his brother.

"We should probably head in; otherwise, he'll come looking for me again," Anya sighed. "Phoebe you look amazing holding a baby!"

Phoebe really was the perfect match for Richard. She was intelligent with quick wit, and she kept Richard on his toes, something few people could do. "I really do, don't I? Phoebe chuckled. "I do believe that this is the happiest baby I've ever had the pleasure of meeting. Here Richard, you have a turn holding him. I'm warning you; you are going to fall in love!"

Richard laughed because he never thought about having children of his own. He enjoyed the way his life had been. But when he met Phoebe, he suddenly felt the urge to settle down. He sat on the couch next to Phoebe, and she passed the baby to him.

"So, Nigel," Phoebe said, watching Nigel pour out steaming cups of tea, "how is Rachel?" Anya's eyes went wide, but not as wide as Nigel's, as he spilled some of the tea.

"Rachel? I don't believe I know a Rachel," Nigel stuttered. "Whoever could you mean?"

"Oh, so this isn't you, sitting at a restaurant with Rachel Evans three weeks ago?" Phoebe's hand slid into her purse, and she pulled out a photograph of Nigel, sitting across the table with a beautiful woman Anya had never seen before. "I don't know how I could have made such a careless mistake. I'm sorry, is that not Rachel? Is it Kate? It's so difficult keeping track of all your girlfriends." Phoebe pulled out several more photographs of Nigel holding hands, kissing, and having dinner with several women who were not Anya." Nigel looked positively livid.

"WHAT?!? Are you accusing me of cheating on Anya? How dare you! I would, I would never do such a thing! Especially while she's pregnant!"

"Oh, but you did, and there is the proof. Now, Richard, I'd like to snuggle the baby some more. He's such a sweetheart!"

Richard looked completely shocked; Phoebe hadn't

mentioned anything about this. They had both suspected Nigel had been cheating on Anya, but he hadn't realized Phoebe went to find proof. Anya sat there, tears in her eyes, but with a calm look on her face. For several months, Anya had suspected that Nigel had been unfaithful, and now with Phoebe's help, she could leave him. She had always liked Phoebe, but at that moment, she loved her.

"Oh, by the way, Anya," I took the liberty to talk to Jax, and here is his official offer to hire you back." Phoebe pulled out a personally written letter from Jax, as well as a contract for hire. "You and this little angel can move in with Richard and me until you find a place of your own. It would be an absolute pleasure to have you." Phoebe beamed as Nigel stormed out of the room.

Richard and Phoebe both looked at Anya. "Anya, I had no idea, Phoebe had managed all of this," Richard said. "I'm so sorry that Nigel was up to no good."

Anya looked at her friends holding onto her sweet little boy, and she started to laugh as she heard Nigel slam the front door as he was shouting at his phone to his brother. "Phoebe, how can I ever repay you?"

"You can say 'yes' to Jax's offer and leave that poor excuse of a husband. These negotiations at work are killing us!" The three friends looked at each other and laughed.

*Acknowledgements*

Writing a book is like putting a jigsaw puzzle together. All the pieces need to fit just "so" otherwise the picture isn't complete and it looks like an utter mess. Without the care, guidance, and support of three people, this book would be an utter mess.

**Scott Hinojos**, without your love and complete support, my dream of being a writer would still be just that, a dream. I know it isn't always easy to read my work, but I really appreciate that you do. Thank you for loving me, just as I am.

**Kelli Cornelius** and **JoAnna Burditt** the pair of you are always quick to proofread and send me notes, even when your own lives are so hectic and full. You constantly amaze me with the insight you provide, as if you can see inside my head. You are both my guiding stars on this journey.

My youngest son **Henry** deserves a special shout out. Henry is wise beyond his years, and quite often sees me sighing heavily in front of my computer. He's quick to remind me to take breaks and offers encouragement along the way. Thank you for all the hugs sweet boy.

A HUGE thank you to anyone who reads my work, especially friends and family. You are all so beautiful. I hope you see yourselves as I see you.

*About the Author*

Stacy Hinojos is a writer of poetry and short fiction. She started writing over thirty years ago, as an outlet for her emotions. "Writing has been both my therapist and my best friend, especially on particularly difficult days. Sitting down with a pen and paper brings me comfort. It's like visiting a trusted friend. By publishing my work, I hope that the reader feels that they are not alone."

She lives in Central Wisconsin with her husband Scott and their son Henry.

For more information about the author visit:
https://www.thesewords.blog/

*Books by Stacy Hinojos*

These Words
A Thousand Melodies
Everything but a Novel

Available on Amazon and wherever fine books are sold.